For Aoife

the Ship's Kitten

Published by Happy Cat Books
An imprint of Catnip Publishing Ltd.
14 Greville Street
London EC1N 8SB

First published in Great Britain 2008

1 3 5 7 9 10 8 6 4 2

A CIP catalogue record for this book is available from the British Library

ISBN   978-1-905117-83-3

Printed in Poland

www.catnippublishing.co.uk

the Ship's Kitten

Illustrated by
Ian P. Benfold Haywood

HAPPY CAT BOOKS

Chapter 1

Somewhere in the world there is a country where the winter is always cold and rainy. Somewhere in that country is an island entirely surrounded by the stormy winter sea.

Somewhere in that island is a small fishing town with shops that shut for the winter but in the summer they sell sticks of rock with your name running through. Somewhere in that town is a harbour where the boats rock and bash against the pier in the squally wind.

Not so long ago in that harbour there was a cardboard box, all damp and sagging from the heavy rain. And somewhere in that cardboard box was a tiny little kitten with no name, and no home, and no idea of what lay outside the box.

The tiny little kitten crouched in a corner and shivered. Hunger pains growled in her tummy. She tried to meow but only made a sniffling sound instead.

The tiny little kitten knew she had to do something. She knew she couldn't crouch in the corner forever.

So she edged towards the middle

of the soggy box to a little gap in the lid where the four flaps didn't quite meet. Gingerly she rose up on her hind legs and poked her tiny pink nose up through the gap.

She took an enormously big
sniff for such a tiny little kitten.

All at once all sorts of lovely,
oily, fishy smells filled her nose.
They made her whiskers quiver
and her tummy rumble. She had
to go and investigate. With a lot
of scrabbling and clawing she
struggled up through the gap.

She took a few wobbly steps,

blinking in the light, and fell off
the box on to the harbour wall.

At once she shrank down and
hissed. The wind hissed back and
blew her ears flat against her tiny
head. The rain hissed back and
drenched her fur. Her tail drooped
down and trailed in a puddle.

Wet and frightened, the kitten
crept back towards the box but
just then – *whoosh!* - a strong gust
of wind sent the box flying off the
harbour wall and into the foaming
sea below.

The kitten battled her way
against the wind over to a wooden
crate where she crouched down
and stared out at the sea.

The dark green sea boiled and
crashed against the wall, fish
glittering like diamonds beneath
the foaming crests of the waves.

She thought she would never see
anything more wonderful than
the fish. The kitten watched the
dancing patterns they made and
forgot all about how cold and wet
she was. But not how hungry.

Boooom! A foghorn blasted out
behind her! She whirled around
and then she saw the boats.
Beautiful painted boats with
funnels and rigging and red plastic
buoys hanging from their sides.

She sat down to wash her paws, and all the while in her imagination she saw a warm bed by the galley stove; kitchen scraps in a porcelain dish bearing the ship's name and high adventure at sea. Despite the rain and the cold the little kitten started to purr. How fine to be a ship's cat!

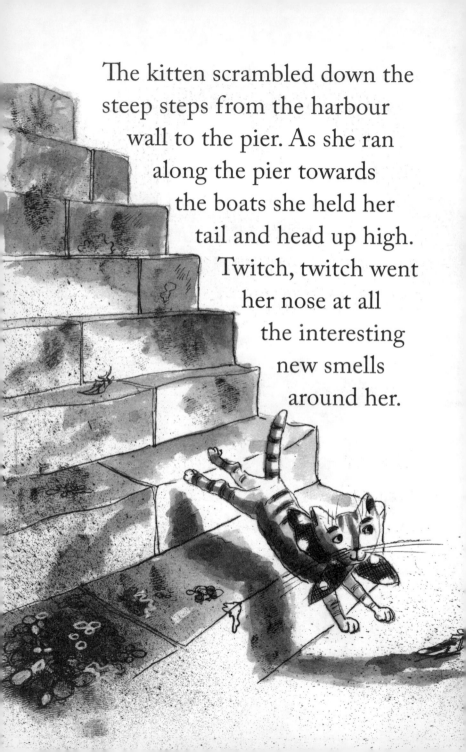

The kitten scrambled down the
steep steps from the harbour
wall to the pier. As she ran
along the pier towards
the boats she held her
tail and head up high.
Twitch, twitch went
her nose at all
the interesting
new smells
around her.

Chapter 2

The kitten went straight for the largest boat of all. This was the blue and white passenger ferry which took people and cars to and from the island. The ferry was brightly lit, waiting in the harbour overnight before an early morning sailing.

What a wonderful life she would
have here, getting scraps from the
cafe and lots of attention from all
the crew and passengers. But at the
top of the gangplank her way was
barred by an enormous black cat.
His back was arched and he was
glaring down at her.

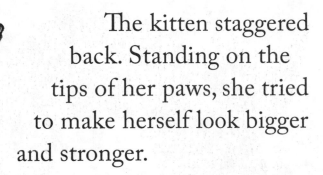

The kitten staggered
back. Standing on the
tips of her paws, she tried
to make herself look bigger
and stronger.

'I don't like the look of you, pal,'
the black cat spat. 'And I'd like to
know where yer think you're going.'
He narrowed his eyes at the kitten.
'This is my patch. I'm ship's cat on
this ferry. Now beat it!'

And he cuffed the kitten so that she rolled over backwards into a puddle.

Bravely the kitten stood back up, smoothed down her whiskers and scampered on to the next boat which was a shining orange lifeboat. This could be an exciting place to live: acts of bravery on the high seas, followed by hot chocolate in a saucer!

But at the top of the gangplank
stood a tough looking marmalade
cat in wellies.

'The name's Magnus and I am ship's cat here. Rescued 23 cats from sinking vessels in me time. You don't cut the mustard. Get outta here!' And he bared his claws menacingly until the kitten slunk away.

Lifting her tail up high she ran on towards a shiny white yacht with varnished wood and brass fittings. Above its deck a green and gold flag flapped loudly in the wind. This looked just the job!

Fresh cream in a gold saucer
brought to her on a silk cushion.
She crouched down ready to spring
onto the deck but there came a
loud hiss from a fur-lined basket.
A sleek white cat uncurled herself
and sidled up to the tiny little
kitten. She circled the kitten, round
and round, and spoke in a long,
slow hiss.

'I, Seleesha, am
ship's cat here. Sooo
sorry but it simply
won't do to have a shabby
little stray on the *Sassorian
Princess*. So scram!' And she
arched her back and hissed at the
kitten until she ran away.

The tiny little kitten sat down on the pier, scratched herself behind one ear and began a thoughtful wash. It wasn't going to be as easy as she thought to become a ship's cat. Perhaps a little scrub up was needed? Then surely she would find a vacancy.

She licked her paws and cleaned behind her ears, before straightening out each and every whisker. She smoothed down her ruffled fur and curled her tail into a perfect arc over her back. At last, sleek and tidy, she marched towards an old fashioned ship with rigging and masts, and cabins made of wood.

As she drew closer she could
hear ropes knocking against the
masts in the wind,with a ringing,
pinging sound that made her heart
beat faster.

How thrilling to race across the ocean, with the sails straining in the wind and the masts creaking. She could eat as many rats as she could catch and always know there'd be more the next day!

But at the top of the gangplank
was a tawny old cat with a black eye
patch. He smelled slightly of rum.

'Be off with yer, ye lubber! I am ship's cat here and I ain't given up the ghost yet.' And the cat took out a long telescope and prodded the kitten back down the gangplank.

Chapter 3

It was nearly dark. Colder, wetter and hungrier than ever the kitten looked up and down the harbour, past the brightly lit bigger boats towards the end of the pier where there were fewer street lamps and more rubbish on the pavement.

There, right at the end of the
harbour, she spotted a tiny little
fishing boat with green and red
flaking paint and the name *Nell*
painted in black on the side. An
old fisherman sat on a large coil of
rope on the deck, mending his nets.

This would have to do. She could
accompany the old fisherman,
who looked kind, when he went
out fishing and on the way back
perhaps he would feed her mackerel
heads, all she could ever want.

But as she
gathered herself to
leap down onto the little
wheelhouse roof something
black and white flashed past
her and landed lightly on the deck.
A cat began to weave in and out of
the fisherman's legs.

Bedgraggled and too tired even to wash, the kitten sat down. Her tummy rumbled so much her whiskers shook.

The wind howled fiercer than ever and the rain lashed down. Miserable, cold, wet and hungry, she crept away from the boats, found the nearest shed and squeezed in through a crack in the door. She crawled into a box, curled up and fell fast asleep.

Meanwhile, the harbour outside was coming alive. The *Radiant Queen*, a huge cruise liner, was slowly and majestically making for the pier, seeking shelter from the growing storm. All seven of its enormous decks were strung with fairy lights and the sound of

an orchestra floated down from its
ballroom to the crowd gathered on
shore to watch its arrival. When
the liner docked some of the
passengers came wobbling down
the gangplank, their legs unused to
dry land after so long at sea.

'A cruise liner! In our harbour!' cried all the ships' cats and they left their boats and gathered to gaze in wonder at the boat. They preened and licked and purred and put on their most winsome expressions – all of them wishing that they could become ship's cat of the *Radiant Queen*.

Suddenly there was a
commotion and a large man with
a huge beard appeared. It was the
Captain and he was shouting and
waving his arms about. He was not
wearing his captain's cap and the
crowd could see his bald patch.

'I'll order a new cap myself then!' The Captain bellowed over his shoulder and marched down the gangplank. At the bottom he shouted above the howling wind, 'Get these cats out of here! I'll have no cats on board my ship!'

The ships' cats slunk away muttering amongst themselves and returned to their boats to sulk.

The Captain strode to the harbour master's office and could be seen and heard through the salt-stained window waving his arms in the air, making squawking noises and pointing wildly at his head.

The harbour master kept a straight face throughout but as soon as the Captain returned to the liner, he locked his office and hurried straight to the *Ferry Inn*.

When they heard his tale the fishermen there laughed until the tears streamed down their faces.

The Captain had been stomping along the deck ordering the passengers not to throw tit-bits to the flock of seagulls that followed the ship when the largest and whitest of the birds had swooped down and flown off with his large, white, beautiful cap!

Chapter 4

The following morning dawned cold and grey but the worst of the storm had passed. Few people were about as the harbour master scurried to the harbour stores. He collected a box containing the captain's brand new cap and hurried aboard the cruise liner with it tucked under his arm.

The Captain had bellowed with anger when the seagull had stolen his cap and he had bellowed again as he told the harbour master all about it. Now he snatched the box angrily from the harbour master, grabbed the cap out of it and set it straight on his head.

By the time the Captain gave the order to cast off a big crowd had gathered on shore to watch the cruise liner leave . The harbour master was there too and the fishermen and all the boat owners and all their cats.

The Captain stood on deck, one hand raised in salute, the brand new cap on his head. He barked orders at his crew and stared straight ahead.

But then an extraordinary thing happened. Despite the freezing wind which had started to swirl sleet and snow around the lights of the cruise liner's seven decks and despite the care needed to guide the stately ship out of the harbour, the Captain smiled!

Indeed, he positively beamed at the crowd, and instead of bellowing out his orders he spoke in a calm voice. He even said please! The crew were astonished, but the Captain went on smiling at everyone. He waved goodbye to the harbour master and the crowd humming a little tune to himself and rocking back and forth on his heels.

What could be making the
Captain so happy? For the very
first time since he'd gone to sea
(a very long time ago) his head
was warm! Even the bald patch
was warm! This made him happier
than he could ever remember. He
took off his cap to wave it at the
harbour master in thanks. But as
he did so he noticed something

inside it and let out a roar.

All eyes shot to the Captain.

The crew stopped what they were doing and stood as still as statues. The crowd fell silent and the ships' cats edged closer to see what was going on.

From out of the cap the Captain
plucked the tiny little kitten. Warm
and snug, she had been sleeping
soundly there ever since she had
crawled in the night before.

The crew hardly dared to

breathe. The harbour master
stepped backwards into
the crowd. The ships' cats
strained so far forward
they all fell off the
harbour wall into the
sea and had to be
fished out by their
owners.

The tiny little kitten was only
half awake. All she knew was that
her lovely warm sleep had been
interrupted. Sleepily, she clambered
up the captain's arm and onto the
top of his head. There she curled
up and went straight back to sleep.

Then the Captain laughed. He
laughed so much the brass buttons
on his uniform flew off and

everyone forgot all the times
he'd ever shouted at them.
He put the cap back on his
head and declared that
the little kitten would be
the first ever ship's cat
on board the *Radiant
Queen*.

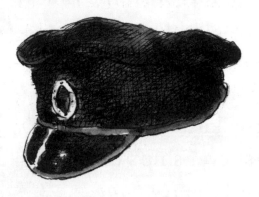

Chapter 5

And so the tiny little kitten who had started out life in a soggy cardboard box left the harbour where the boats rock and bash against the pier in the squally wind. She sailed away from the island which is entirely surrounded by the stormy winter sea and said goodbye to the country where the winter is always cold and rainy. And she went out into the big wide world on the cruise liner *Radiant Queen*, eating the very best, tastiest tit-bits straight from the Captain's table.

And she leads a very fine life
indeed.

The Princess
and the Unicorn

Wendy Blaxland

No one believes in unicorns any more. Except Princess Lily, that is.
So when the king falls ill and the only thing that can cure him is
the magic of a unicorn, it's up to her to find one.
But can Lily find a magical unicorn in time?

Becky was cross with her little brother. 'If you don't leave me alone,' she said to him, 'I'll put a spell on you!' But she didn't mean to make him disappear!

THE MERMAID'S TAIL

RAEWYN CAISLEY

Crystal longs to be a mermaid.
Her mother makes her a flashing silver tail. But it isn't like
being a proper mermaid. Then one night Crystal wears her
tail to bed...

Jock can make a special sound like a duck!
If you can learn to make it too you can help Jock rescue the
little duck from the duck hunter. Quick, before it's too late!

David's had a party invitation!
It's a dressing-up party and he's going to go as a fox. But
when he arrives he can see he's made a mistake in choosing
his costume. Can he still fit in with the party theme and
have fun?

Nicholas Nosh is the littlest pirate in the world. He's not allowed to go to sea. 'You're too small,' said his dad. But when the fierce pirate Captain Red Beard kidnaps his family, Nicholas sets sail to rescue them!

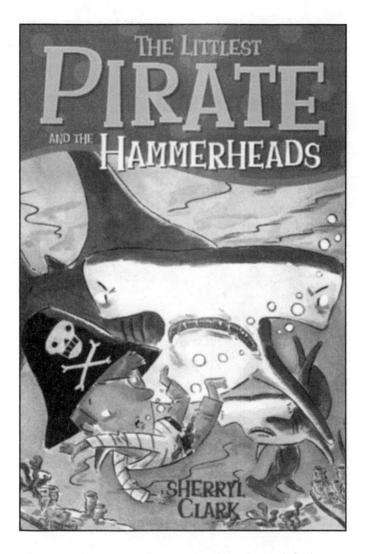

Nicholas Nosh, the littlest pirate in the world, has to rescue
his family's treasure which has been stolen by Captain
Hammerhead. But how can he outwit the sharks that are
guarding Captain Hammerhead's ship?

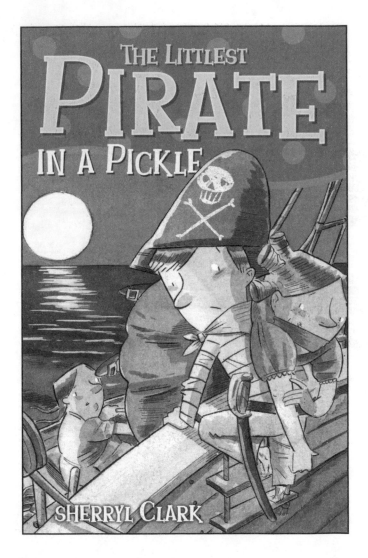

THE LITTLEST PIRATE IN A PICKLE

SHERRYL CLARK

Nicholas Nosh is teased by his cousin Primrose for being so small. But when Captain Manners of the Jolly Dodger kidnaps her, Nicholas shows just how brave a little pirate he can be!

Nobody is better at being bad than Buster Reed – he flicks
paint, says rude words to girls, sticks chewing gum under
the seats and wears the same socks for weeks at a time.
Naturally no one wants to know him. But Buster has a
secret – he would like a friend to play with.
How will he ever manage to find one?

when Anna Slept Over

Jane Godwin

Josie is Anna's best friend. Anna has played at Josie's house,
she's even stayed for dinner, but she has never slept over.
Until now...